KU-738-606

THE HUGE BAG OF
WORRIES

THE HUGE BAG OF
WORRIES

By Virginia Ironside
Illustrations by Frank Rodgers

HODDER
Wayland

an imprint of Hodder Children's Books

For Finn and Will Russell-Cobb

Text copyright © 1996 Virginia Ironside
Illustrations copyright © 1996 Frank Rodgers

First published in Great Britain in 1996 by
Macdonald Young Books

Reprinted in 2001 by Hodder Wayland,
an imprint of Hodder Children's Books

Hodder Children's Books
A division of Hodder Headline Ltd
338 Euston Road, London NW1 3BH

All rights reserved

The right of Virginia Ironside to be identified as the author of this Work and the right of
Frank Rodgers to be identified as the illustrator of this Work has been asserted by them
in accordance with the Copyright, Designs and Patents Act 1988.

Printed in Hong Kong

British Library Cataloguing in Publication Data available.

ISBN: 0 7500 2124 1

Jenny had always been happy. She had a lovely mum and dad, a great brother (well, most of the time…), she had a best friend at school and she liked her teacher. And then, of course, there was Loftus.

But recently she had been getting gloomier and gloomier.
It wasn't just one thing; it was everything.

She worried that she
was getting too fat,

that Loftus had fleas

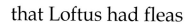

and that her best friend
was going away.

She worried that she was getting bad marks at school and she thought she heard someone whispering about her in the playground…

she worried when her mum and dad had an argument…

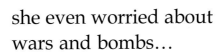

she even worried about wars and bombs…

until one day she woke to find…

... a HUGE BAG OF WORRIES.

The bag followed her everywhere...

to school,

to swimming,

to the toilet,

and it stuck by her even
when she was watching TV.

She tried ignoring it…
but it didn't work.

She tried throwing it away…   but it always came back.

She tried to lock it out,

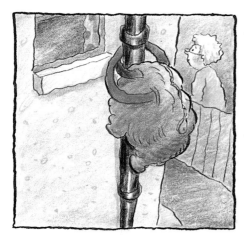

but when she got back to her bedroom, there it was, waiting for her.

It was like a horrible shadow she couldn't get rid of.

What could she do?

She asked her brother for help. But he was busy with his computer game, and all he said was: "I don't know what you are talking about. *I* don't have any worries."

After that she didn't feel like asking anyone else. She knew she'd only feel stupid.

Mum would probably say: "You've got no worries that I can see. You're a lucky girl. You've got your health, your friends, your family – what more do you want?" So she decided not to tell her.

Dad might know what to do.
But then she thought again.
No. Dad had enough
worries of his own.
She couldn't ask him.

Every day things got worse.

The bag got bigger...   and bigger...

and bigger.

She couldn't sleep because it kept tossing and turning
beside her all night.

To make matters worse, the bag dragged around her feet so much when she was walking to school that she was late and the teacher was cross.

Jenny couldn't tell her what had happened, and anyway she knew what she would say: "You've got too many worries! In future, leave that bag at home!"

When Jenny told her best friend about the bag, she suggested that Jenny locked it up in a cupboard and tried not to think about it. "That's what I do," she said.

But it just didn't work.

Even Loftus couldn't help.

He tried his best and
barked like mad,

but the bag stood its ground.

One morning Jenny woke up, got dressed and walked down
the road. She'd had enough. The tears started rolling down
her cheeks. She sat on a garden wall and put her head in her
hands. She thought she'd have to live with the bag forever.

Then she heard a voice and, looking up, she saw the kindly face of the old lady who lived next door.

"Goodness!" said the old lady. "What on earth is that HUGE bag of worries?"

Through her tears, Jenny explained how it had followed her for weeks, and got bigger and bigger, and just wouldn't go away.

"Now let's just open it up and see what's inside," said the old lady.

But Jenny said she couldn't. If she opened the bag, the worries might jump out and who knew what might happen then.

"Nonsense," said the old lady firmly. "There's nothing a worry hates more than being seen. If you have any worries, however small, the secret is to let them out slowly, one by one, and show them to someone else. They'll soon go away."

So Jenny opened the bag.

The old lady sorted the worries into groups.

Jenny was astonished to see how small they looked when they were out in the open.

Half the worries disappeared because lots of worries just hate the light of day.

As for the rest, the old lady put some in her shopping basket to deal with herself;

some she sent packing because she said they belonged to other people;

some she just blew a kiss to;

and some she said were worries that everyone had,
even Jenny's family, her friends and her teacher.

And as for the bag…

Here are some more picture books by Hodder Wayland for you to enjoy:

The Jolly Witch
Written by Dick King-Smith · Illustrated by Frank Rodgers
Mrs Jolly is a school caretaker by day and a witch by night! She uses her magic powers to help her clean the school – until one special night when she casts a rather unusual spell on the vacuum cleaner.

Mrs Jollipop
Written by Dick King-Smith · Illustrated by Frank Rodgers
The lovable witch Mrs Jolly is back! But this time she's a lollipop lady, which is why the children call her Mrs Jollipop! Mrs Jollipop can't resist using her magic powers on her lollipop. So it doesn't always say 'STOP CHILDREN' and it doesn't always stay firmly on the ground (and nor does Mrs Jolly!).

Grimbledon Zoo is Closing Down
Written and illustrated by Keith Brumpton
Grimbledon Zoo is closing down and there's to be an auction of all the animals. Tina takes the hyena, Brian Ryan takes the lion – but some of the animals prove to be a bit of a problem. Can the zoo be saved after all?

Archie The Ugly Dinosaur
Written by Christina Butler · Illustrated by Val Biro
Archie is very small – for a dinosaur. To make matters worse, he starts to grow funny little spikes. His friends laugh at him so he runs away. Then they begin to worry. Have the Tyrannosaurus Rexes captured him? But they needn't have feared because Archie has become a beautiful bird – an Archaeopteryx!

For further information about these and other books, write to:
The Sales Department, Hodder Children's Books,
338 Euston Road, London NW1 3BH